Onyx Kids

School Days

Book Seven

The Prank War

By Rita Onyx

Onyx Star Publishing, LLC
Delaware, USA

To Mirthell, Shasha, Shiloh, Shalom,
Sinead
who without them this wouldn't be
possible.

Thank You

Table of Contents

Chapter One
He's baaaack....

`Code Pentagon`

The code went out to the group of five friends in their group chat. The text meant that they needed to head over to Evan's secret lab ASAP.

Shiloh got it as he was getting ready for school. He heard the ding of his phone go off as he was brushing his teeth. He walked back to his room with his toothbrush in his hands, mouth full of toothpaste and spit.

All of a sudden it felt like he walked into an invisible forcefield in his doorway. His toothbrush was jerked out of his mouth and his face was smeared with toothpaste. He felt a light film all over his body and couldn't shake it off.

He heard his sister Shasha laughing. "I know it's an oldie, but it's still a goodie. Plastic wrap in the doorway gets the job done! Happy April Fools' Day!" She was talking to her phone.

"You put that on Instagram?!"

"Of course not. I put it on TikTok," Shasha said with a dismissive shake of her head. "I have to grow my followers."

"Shasha, not this again! You know I'll get you back so why do you keep doing this?"

"Are you saying, you're starting a prank war?" Shasha her left eyebrow up in challenge.

"I didn't start this, but I'll finish it." Shiloh crossed his arms and stared her down.

"Bro, you watch too many action movies. No one's gonna care about my little TikTok vi—
I can't believe it got thirty thousand views already!"

"Shasha delete it now!"

"Nope!" She ran down the hall and back into her room.

His phone dinged again which reminded him what he was on his way to do. He read the text and muttered, "What? I thought it was over."

Shiloh to Evan:

> Bruh, I thought it
> was over. What
> happened?

Evan to Shiloh:

> You'll see when you
> get here. It could
> be nothing, but I
> doubt it. It looks
> like The Watcher is
> back.

This sent chills down Shiloh's spine. He and his friends had a few months of no problems with The Watcher. It wasn't even that they had any problems with The Watcher because all he, or maybe she, did was...watch. But that was unnerving in of itself. To be watched and not know who was doing the watching.

Desirae to Shiloh:

> Did you get it?

Shiloh to Desirae:

> Evan's text? Yup.
> He told me he's
> back.

Desirae to Shiloh:

```
I wonder what this
means?
```

As Shiloh was writing back Desirae, he got a text from Roxy.

Roxy to Shiloh:

```
I can't believe
he's back.
```

Shiloh to Desirae:

```
I have no idea.
```

Shiloh to Roxy:

```
I know!
```

Shiloh thought that he was doing a great job of juggling both conversations. *Not so bad. I mean girls do this all the time, so I don't see what's so hard.*

Desirae to Shiloh:

```
I mean what could
he want after all
this time? It's
been months. I
wonder who it is?
```

> Who do you think it
> is? What does this
> all mean??

Roxy to Shiloh:

> Do you want to meet
> by your locker
> before we go down
> to the lab or are
> you meeting
> Desirae?

Shiloh walked into the hallway as he was trying to text both Desirae and Roxy. He was so engrossed with his texts he didn't notice her.

"What are you doing?" She grabbed the phone and read the texts.

"Code Pentagon?" She looked up confused then continued to read. "Ohhh, you dirty dog. You have two girlfriends! Wait till mom and dad hear about this." She tried to leave the bathroom.

Shiloh blocked her. "They're not my girlfriends. They're just friends and happen to be girls." He made a praying hand gesture. "Please don't

11

make this a big deal and tell mom and dad. They'll want to invite them over and talk with them and be all weird when all we are JUST FRIENDS."

He didn't mean to yell at the last bit, but he was already a little nervous with The Watcher being back and trying to keep Shasha from going downstairs and writing back Desirae and Roxy.

His phone went off again with two dings almost simultaneously. He tried to grab his phone again from Shasha.

"Let's see who it is now? Maybe it's another girl!" Shasha laughed as she ducked around him and ran down the hall with his phone.

"Shasha! Give it back!" Shiloh yelled.

"Shasha and Shiloh! We don't have time for playing around this morning. We have to go! Hurry up and come down and eat your breakfast," Mom called from downstairs.

That stopped them both in their tracks.

"Shasha! Give it back, *now*." Shiloh hoped he looked serious enough to scare her.

"Alright, alright. I was just playing. You do know it's April Fools' Day today right? Too bad you can't take a joke," she shrugged and tossed him back his phone as she walked past him back into the bathroom.

"Yes, but this isn't a prank. You're just being annoying." Shiloh breathed a sigh of relief and looked down at his phone to read the texts.

Desirae to Shiloh:

Hello?

Roxy to Shiloh:

. . .

How was he supposed to reply to three periods? He thought briefly of asking Shasha but quickly dismissed that thought. She'd probably tease him some more and really annoy him. He decided he wouldn't overthink it.

Shiloh to Desirae:

> Yes.

Shiloh to Roxy:

> I have no clue.

There that took care of it...or so he thought.

Desirae to Shiloh:

> Took you long enough. If you didn't want to text right now you could've just told me. What kind of answer is "yes"? That tells me nothing. Whatever I'll see you at school.

Roxy to Shiloh:

> Ok, I get it.
> That's fine. We
> don't have to meet
> at your locker. See
> you in the lab.

Shiloh realized too late that he had mixed up his responses. He cringed thinking of seeing them in less than an hour. *Maybe I could say I'm sick...* He shrugged off that thought. He would go to school and face the music.

How bad could it be?

~

Two stony faces greeted him in Evan's lab half an hour later. Shiloh cleared his throat in nervousness.

"Is there something wrong?" Evan whispered to Desirae. He noticed that she looked annoyed but couldn't figure out why.

"No. Nothing at all," she said with her arms folded.

"Are you sure? You and Roxy look like you guys got in a fight or something," Max said. He had been watching them too.

Roxy and Desirae looked at each other with a quizzical look on their face and then as if a lightbulb went off in both of their heads at the same time they both whipped around and gave Shiloh a hard stare.

Both Evan and Max saw this and also realized it had to do with Shiloh, so they joined in and glared at him too.

"Guys, can we focus please? You know, Code Pentagon, The Watcher. Guys?" Shiloh tried to get them back on track.

16

Evan stared for another few seconds before he turned to the rest of the group. "He's right. I called you all down here to show you this." He pointed to the table in the middle of the room. On the table was a puzzle that had been put together.

"You brought us down here so we can work on puzzles? I know you don't have a lot of friends Evan, and maybe this is why—

"Max! I obviously didn't bring you down here to assemble puzzles. Look at the picture!" Evan was exasperated and a little embarrassed by what Max said. Sure, he didn't have a lot of friends but that was because most kids were into things that didn't matter like selfies and TikTok. He was interested in the mysteries of science and now the mystery of The Watcher.

All five them crowded around the table and looked at the puzzle. The picture was of a slimy green splat.

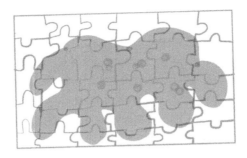

"This is actually kind of..." Roxy's voice faded out

"I'll say it. Gross! Why would you buy a booger puzzle?! Is this an April Fools' joke?" Desirae said disgustedly.

"Look, I'm sure Evan had his reasons for buying this puzzle," Shiloh tried to defend his friend. "But for real though, it is kinda gross. Couldn't you have bought another one that was less...weird." He patted Evan's shoulder.

Evan rolled his eyes. "Guys, I didn't buy this. This is what The Watcher left along with a note. I'll read it."

18

I let you five have your fun.
Now it's time to make you run.
Better get to class on time.
So you can watch me unleash the
slime.
Try and stop it if you dare.
But the consequences won't be fair.
You'll get the blame from the entire
school
Too bad cause this is just the start of
April Fool
I'm on the attack
And yes that means...I'm back.
-The Watcher

"That was a lame poem. Dr. Seuss had better rhymes," Max scoffed.

"What does he mean 'get to class on time and watch him unleash the slime'?" Shiloh wondered.

"I think it means someone is going to get slimed," Evan answered. "I wonder who it will be?"

"We have to put ourselves in The Watcher's shoes. If I was going to slime someone here at school who would it be?" Evan mused.

The five of them paused for a second to consider and a flash of understanding went through them like lightening.

They all cried out at the same time, "Miss Suffering!"

Chapter Two
A Slimy Situation

The five of them ran out of the lab and upstairs into the main hall of the school. Students were still milling about on their way to class. As they ran towards Miss Suffering's classroom they pushed people out of the way.

"Move people! We got an emergency!" Evan shouted as he led the way.

"Miss Suffering we'll save you!" Desirae said as they got to Miss Suffering's classroom and threw the door open and burst inside, jarring the classmates who were already seated. Miss Suffering, who was standing next to her desk, was also startled and had let out a small scream.

Pulling herself together and patting the rock-hard bun on her head, she scolded, "Save me from what? Teaching you bad-mannered kids all day? I would have you know, you all

21

know," she narrowed her eyes at them and the rest of the class who were watching the spectacle, "No one bursts into my room except my mother. In fact, she did it last night, at midnight, to remind me to do the dishes. Unfortunately, she forgot that she lives in *my* house and I will do the dishes when I want!" She abruptly stopped and looked up to see everyone staring at her. Embarrassed by her rant, she refocused on the students, "This unruly behavior will not be tolerated. There is no running in the halls and definitely no running in my class."

"But– Shiloh tried to explain.

"Shiloh find your seat. All of you find your seat and the rest of you get to your homerooms. This is ridiculous," she continued to reprimand.

Shiloh and his friends looked at each other and shrugged.

Roxy whispered, "Maybe The Watcher was just messing with us."

"You're probably right," Evan whispered back.

Miss Suffering cleared her throat loudly. Shiloh and Desirae quickly got to their seat. Evan, Max, and Roxy went to their homeroom with Mr. Thomas.

"Ok, now that we're all settled. Let me take roll–

RING

A ringing went off in the classroom. The class was silent as they looked around to see whose phone could've went off. Everyone knew that you had to have your phone on mute or it would be taken away.

"Whose phone is that?!" Miss Suffering yelled. Everyone stayed silent.

RING

"I see you guys are covering for each other," she walked down the aisle of desks and eyed each student carefully.

RING

"AH HA!" She whirled around and slammed her hand on the desk behind her.

The student crouched down and pointed at the cabinet above her. "It's not mine," she said.

Miss Suffering realized that she was in fact right. The ringing was coming from a cabinet she rarely used. "Who put their phone in there? Normally, I would congratulate whoever it was on putting it away, but it really should be set to silent so that it doesn't disturb the class." She rolled her eyes as she reached for the cabinet door. "Why do you guys do things half-baked. I'll walk you through how to–

What happened next would live on in Cornerstone infamy. Shiloh watched it as if it was in slow motion. He had an inkling that something wasn't right when he saw that the phone was in the cabinet, so he had secretly whipped out his phone to record what he knew was about to happen.

As Miss Suffering opened the door a bucket of green slime dropped forward and splashed in her face.

She screamed, the girls in the class shrieked, and the guys shouted "Oooooohhhhh!"

"Someone get me a paper towel!"

No one moved. They were in shock, and a little grossed out. They didn't want to get any slime on them.

"I'll get it myself. Why would I think you guys would be of any help!" She moved over to the cabinet she used for paper towels. As she opened it another bucket of slime smacked her in the face.

She sputtered, "I....can't....I.....WHAT IS HAPPENING?!" She stood there covered in slime.

Mr. Thomas ran in the room with his class right behind him. "What's going on in here?" Evan, Roxy, and Max looked at each other and then at Shiloh and Desirae.

"Tom! Look what they did to me!" She cried. She ran to his arms, but he held her back.

"Why don't we get you cleaned up first," He said awkwardly. "And what about the rule of PDA Agony?" He whispered then cleared his throat. Everyone knew that Mr. Thomas and Miss Suffering were a couple but they didn't admit to the students. When they were at school they kept it very under the radar.

She straightened up immediately. "Do you think I care? Just. Get. Me. Out. Of. Here." As she turned to leave the students parted like the Red Sea to let her pass and so they wouldn't get the goo on them.

After they left the students stayed quiet for a second, but then they started to snicker. The snickers turned into guffaws and the next minute there were howls of laughter. Some of them started to mimic her opening the cabinet and getting sprayed with slime which made them all laugh even harder.

The only people who weren't laughing were Shiloh, Desirae, Evan, and Roxy. Max had joined in the revelry and was crying with laughter too.

"Max! How can you laugh at a time like this?" Roxy admonished.

"How can you not laugh? Miss Suffering had it coming to her. She is so mean! A little slime never hurt anybody."

Roxy looked like she had been slapped. "How could you say that? No one deserves to have slime thrown in their face. How would you like it if someone did that to you?"

Evan, Shiloh, and Desirae raised their eyebrows and gave each other looks as they listened to them argue.

"I wouldn't care. It's just slime," Max said snidely.

"Oh really? We'll see about that." Roxy stomped to the counter and got some slime and smeared it on his cheek.

"What did you do that for?"

"I thought it didn't matter."

"You know what I meant, Roxy. Yuck! If it was anyone but you I'd— He was about to go on but stopped himself before he did. He looked slightly embarrassed by his admission.

Shiloh had heard enough. "Ok you two. Can we focus please? I happen to have it all on my phone as evidence. We need to get to the bottom of who put it there. Clearly, it's The Watcher but we need to figure out who it is and stop them now. If this is just the beginning can you imagine what else he has in store?"

"Why do we need to stop him?" Max said as he continued to wipe his face.

"You are so...," Roxy sneered.

"I'm just saying that maybe he's doing what we all dreamt of doing. How many of us have ever wanted to put Miss Suffering in her place?"

Roxy was about to open her mouth, but was interrupted by Evan.

"You're right, Max. You know, you missed a spot right there." Evan pointed at the side of his face. "You should go get cleaned up too."

Max gave a frustrated look to Roxy before he stomped off.

"Bruh, there wasn't anything on his face," Shiloh said confused.

"I know. I wanted to get him to leave for a second. Don't you think it's interesting that he's all for this? He has no problem with what happened."

"And?" Desirae questioned.

"And, I think that he's The Watcher."

"Whoa, what?" Roxy was stunned. "Just because he thinks it's funny doesn't mean that he's The Watcher. I'm with him all the time. There's no way that it's him."

No one said anything. "Guys? Shiloh? You don't really think it's him, do you?" Roxy asked.

Shiloh raised his eyebrows and shrugged. "I gotta admit it's a little fishy."

"It's not him," Roxy stood her ground.

"Look, no one's saying for sure that it's him. I think we're all a little on edge," Desirae put her arm around Roxy's shoulder and gave Shiloh and Evan a look that made them quiet down.

The door to the classroom opened and Miss Suffering came back in looking a little green, literally. The slime had stained her skin a tint of green and her normally plain gray dress was patterned with dried splotches of slime. Her face was green, but her ears were red. Shiloh thought it reminded him of a cartoon character. He wouldn't have been surprised if steam started to radiate from them.

Before she was able to speak, the bell rang, letting them out of class. But no one dared move because she was blocking the doorway.

"Um, Miss Suffering, I'm going to be late for art?" A lone voice from the back said softly.

"Well, we wouldn't want you to be late for art now would we?" She said in a sugary tone.

You could cut the tension with a butter knife. Miss Suffering moved to the side. "Ok, everyone get to your class except Shiloh. You stay."

Everyone looked at Shiloh who looked panicked. The rest of the class quickly got their things and headed out.

The class emptied and it was just Shiloh and Miss Suffering.

Chapter Three
If You Give A Mouse A Cookie

"Hand me your phone," Miss Suffering ordered.

Shiloh didn't want to give her his phone because he thought he might not get it back.

"Why? I didn't have anything to do with what happened. I mean it. I had zero to do with it. I'm so sorry that happened to you."

"Sure, I believe you. Even though you were very quick to whip out your phone as if you knew it was going to happen. *I'm watching you.*" She paused and looked him squarely in the eye. "Ok, if you don't want to give it to me that's fine, but I want you to delete the video. There's no way I want this on Tic Tac or You Too."

Shiloh was confused, "You mean TikTok or YouTube? Don't you have any social media accounts?" He'd been so caught up with what happened that he didn't even think about uploading it.

"Of course I do, I have MySpace. Apparently, all the cool people are there. If you go on my profile you'll hear me singing my favorite song. I get comments all the time of people saying they've never heard a voice like mine before and that I put goats to shame. If you post this and it goes viral I'll lose my cool status."

Now that she mentioned it, he realized it really could go viral. She must have seen the idea take root on his face because she started to look alarmed. "Now Shiloh, you wouldn't want to embarrass your favorite teacher would you?"

"No, I'd never embarrass Mr. Thomas."

She scowled. "Delete that this instant!" She marched over to him.

"Ok, ok." Shiloh pressed delete with her looking over his shoulder.

"There. That wasn't so bad was it?"
She looked smug. "No get to class!"

Shiloh ran out of the room and to his
next class.

~

Code Pentagon
meeting at lunch.

Shiloh and the crew got the text
from Evan and were now assembling
at a small table at lunch.

Desirae asked, "What did Miss
Suffering want? Did she think you're
the one who did it?"

"She said I whipped out my phone
before it happened as if I knew it
what was about to go down."

"That's kinda true Shiloh. How did
you know?" Desirae questioned.

"What? I didn't know. The only thing
I knew was that The Watcher
warned us and then I heard a weird
ringing. I have never heard a phone

ringing in a cabinet before. I just put two and two together. Besides, we know who probably set this whole thing up." He glanced at Max.

Max caught the glance. "Hey, why'd you look at me? I didn't do it."

"Yeah but you seemed far too happy with what happened," Evan stated.

Roxy intervened, "Look guys, let's stop pointing fingers and just try and stop whatever happens next. Evan, did you get another clue?"

"Yeah, I did. I didn't have time to put it together yet so let's do it here." Evan spread a new puzzle on the table. "While you guys put it together I'll read the note."

What happens if you give a mouse a cookie
Why don't we have a little looky
Screaming and running sounds about right
I'll be watching and laughing at the chaotic sight.

"Done," Desirae said.

The five of them looked at the new puzzle. It was a mouse nibbling at a cookie.

"Okay...now what? Are we supposed to be looking for a mouse?" Max asked.

"Let's reason this out, where would we find mice? The basement. Maybe we should head to the basement," Evan said.

"First of all, I'm not going to the basement to look for rats!" Desirae exclaimed.

"This isn't a picture of a rat, this is clearly a mouse," Shiloh stated what he thought was obvious.

"I don't care! They're all the same to me." Desirae folded her arms in front of her and shivered.

"If you want to see a rat, I'll show you a picture of a rat," Shiloh laughed and started scrolling.

"Don't you dare! Shiloh if you show me a picture of a nasty—

"Uh, hey guys. Guys!" Max shouted to get their attention. "I don't think we have to go to the basement to find some mice." He pointed to students screaming and jumping on the tables.

Dozens of mice were running across the cafeteria floor and scrambling up chairs and even pant legs. Miss Suffering who was walking with Mr. Thomas threw her tray causing her soup to splash all over him. She ran onto a table and screamed. Mr. Thomas tried to run away as well

but slipped on the soup and landed
on his butt.

Other students tried to use their
trays to swat at them to keep them
off the tables. The lunch ladies
abandoned their post and ran down
the hall, hairnets and all.

Shiloh, once again, captured it all on
his phone. "This day is awesome! I
think I like this Watcher." He
laughed at the mayhem.

"Shiloh! This isn't funny! Do
something!" Desirae pleaded.

"Let's throw our food in the corner
and maybe they'll all go after it,"
Shiloh suggested.

39

The five of them began to throw their food in the corner. Other students saw it and misread their actions and started throwing their food too, causing a huge food fight on top of the already crazy situation. Food was everywhere.

"Well that didn't work," Shiloh shrugged.

"You think?" Roxy said exasperated. "Let's get out of here. On three let's make a run for it. One, Two–

Before she could even get to three the rest of them took off. "Hey! Wait for me!" Roxy yelled after them.

~

Shiloh and Evan leaned against the lockers while Max sat down on the floor. Desirae and Roxy hugged themselves and kept swatting at imaginary mice on their shoulders.

"I don't know how you can sit down on the floor," Roxy said to Max.

"Believe me, they're not here. They are where the food is. Besides I'm tired. I've never run that fast in my life!" He panted.

"We need to figure this out. I don't know how this day could get any worse," Desirae said.

"I don't know. These pranks are kind of funny. I'm actually enjoying it. I want to see what he does next," Shiloh said.

"What? Maybe you really are The Watcher," Roxy said annoyed at his flippant attitude.

"Me? Just cause I think it's funny?"

"That's what you guys said about Max," she countered.

"What?" Max stood up. "You guys thought it was me? When did you have your little meeting to discuss?" He turned to Roxy. "Why didn't you tell me that they think I'm a suspect?"

"I told them it wasn't you," Roxy defended herself.

"You know what, I gotta get to my next class. See you guys later." Max stormed off.

"See, that's what happens when we start pointing fingers. We're all on the same team so let's start acting like it and actually try to do something about this," Evan said frustratingly.

As he opened his locker to get his books for the next class, puzzle pieces fell out.

"Oh no! It's not what I think it is, is it? Please tell me you actually do like puzzles," Shiloh pleaded with Evan.

"Sorry but no. It's another clue," Evan sighed.

"Let's pretend we didn't see it," Desirae suggested. "If there's something worse than mice, I really don't want to know. In fact, why don't we all go home early?"

"Get a hold of yourself Des!" Roxy said as she shook Desirae's shoulders. "We can handle this. We can stop this. We just have to be one step ahead of him."

"She's right." Evan agreed.

"You're right! We can do this. After all, it was just slime...and mice. No biggie." Desirae tried to play it off. It would've been more convincing if she wasn't looking around paranoid as she said it.

"Let's put this together quickly and Shiloh you read the note this time," Evan ordered.

Is it only a skunk that can bring the funk?
Is it only poo that stinks up the loo?
Try not to gag at this next one
Because this one won't be as fun

They finished putting the puzzle together and saw it was a picture of a skunk.

"I have to say, it looks pretty life-like," Shiloh said as he admired the picture.

"Why did he say it won't be as fun. None of this has been fun," Desirae complained.

"Should we search the bathrooms?" Roxy asked.

"I feel like that's too obvious. We're about to head back to class so I feel like he would do something in class."

"We should split up and search the classrooms quickly before lunch period is over," Shiloh suggested.

"And search for what?" Evan asked.

"We'll know when we see it," Shiloh answered.

"Good idea. I'll go with Shiloh," Desirae volunteered and hooked her arm around his.

Evan looked a little hurt. "I guess it's you and me Roxy. We'll meet back here in fifteen minutes." They walked away together to search the other side of the school.

Shiloh watched them go. If he really thought about it, he would've rather been with Roxy but there was no time to think about that stuff...at least that's what he thought.

"Why did your text sound so weird this morning?" Desirae asked as they walked quickly to the first classroom to search.

"My sister was annoying me this morning and she made me mix up my texts," Shiloh answered as he opened and closed drawers.

"You were texting someone else at the same time?" Desirae asked as she closed the cabinet a little too hard.

"Yeah, I was also chatting with Roxy," Shiloh said unaware of how Desirae was looking at him.

"I see."

Shiloh heard the change in her tone and turned to face her. "I didn't find anything here. Let's go to the next one."

"Sure."

"Did you find anything?" He asked.

"Nope."

Shiloh was confused as to why he was only getting one-word answers. "Are you mad at me?"

"No."

"Are you sure?"

"Why would I be mad?"

"I have no idea." He was truly confused.

They searched the next classroom in silence. The tension was thick.

"Des, look if I did something, I'm sorry." Shiloh didn't know what else to say. He couldn't figure out girls.

Silence.

"Look, if you're still upset then I don't know what to tell you. I thought we were all friends and I can't believe you'd be mad at me for talking to another friend. Besides Evan likes you a lot and I don't want to get in the way of that." He knew he probably shouldn't have told her that last part because Evan would be mad, but it was so obvious that he felt like she knew anyway. Might as well get it out in the open.

Silence.

Shiloh walked over to where Desirae was. She hadn't been paying attention to what Shiloh was saying. She was staring at something in a drawer.

"Des?"

"Look at this! It's a wrapper for a stink bomb!" She held up the wrapper.

"I didn't find any stink bombs in here though," Shiloh said.

"No, but now we know what we're looking for," she said triumphantly.

"I'll text Evan," Shiloh said as he got out his phone and took a picture of the wrapper in Desirae's hand.

"Ready to go to the next one?" Shiloh asked, "Or are you still mad?"

"I'm not mad."

"Did you hear what I said earlier?"

"About what?" She asked.

"Nothing. It was nothing. Let's go," Shiloh was relieved. Maybe she didn't need to know about Evan right now.

~

"I got a text from Shiloh. Looks like we're looking for a stink bomb," Evan announced to Roxy.

"I've never seen one before. I've read about them, but I've never seen one in person, much less smelled one," Roxy said.

"I haven't either and I don't want to. Let's hope we find it before it goes off."

They kept searching through the drawers, desks, cabinets, and garbage cans in each room as they went down the hall.

"Do you like Desirae?" Roxy asked.

Evan suddenly felt hot and off balance. "Why...why would you...ask that?" He tried to look composed.

"Because it's the worst kept secret in the world."

"Who told you?" Evan demanded. "Shiloh? I told him not to tell anyone."

"You told me."

"What? I never told you anything."

"You tell everyone by your face and the way you act around her. Plus, you basically told me just now too. It's ok, I won't tell anyone who doesn't know by now. I think the janitors may not know...yet." She laughed.

"That's funny. That's real funny. It's obvious you like Max so I guess we're even."

"What? I don't like Max."

"With the way you defended him, I think you do."

"He's my friend. Friends defend friends."

"Sure. Whatever," Evan looked bored of the conversation.

"I'm serious. I don't like Max I like—

"I'm waiting," Evan said mockingly.

"Never mind. Let's just look for the stink bomb ok?" Roxy turned away embarrassed.

"Sorry Roxy. I didn't mean to embarrass you."

"It's ok. I just…"

"Ewwww….what's that smell?" Someone in the hallway shouted.

Evan and Roxy looked up at the same time and dashed out of the room. As soon as they opened the door, they were hit with a stench so thick you could taste it.

Both of them hid their noses and mouths inside their shirt to try and not breathe so much of it in, but it was no use. They ran to the closest exit.

Outside was pandemonium as students spilled out of the school coughing and gagging.

Evan and Roxy looked for Shiloh and Desirae. As they were walking around the crowd they bumped into Max.

"Isn't this cool?" His voice was muffled behind his shirt as he tried to avoid the intense smell.

"No, it isn't cool. This could make people actually sick. It's like I don't even know you," Roxy said. "Come on Evan, let's go find them."

"Hey! Rox!" Max called behind them.

"Don't you think you were a little hard on him?" Evan said to Roxy as they kept walking?

"No and I'm starting to wonder if it really is him. He doesn't seem to care that this whole day has been a hot mess."

"Yeah, but guys don't really make big deals over things."

"Are you saying girls do?" Roxy said surprised.

"No, what I'm saying is—

"What are you saying?" Roxy asked with her arms folded.

"Hey there's Shiloh and Desirae!" Evan called out to them. Relieved to have avoided the conversation.

The four of them met up and walked to the edge of the front yard.

"That was disgusting!" Desirae squealed. "I can't believe I could taste it!"

"We were so close!" Shiloh exclaimed.

"Did you guys see where it went off?" Roxy asked.

"Yes, I actually got it on my phone," Shiloh explained. "We happened to go into Mr. Thomas' classroom and he and Miss Suffering were in there eating their lunch. I guess they wanted to avoid the lunchroom after the mice. I told them that we were looking for extra pens and paper and we asked if we could look in his room. The first drawer we opened must have triggered it. Something sprayed and all of a sudden my eyes started to water and I wanted to gag. I tried to tell Desirae not to open the drawer close to Mr. Thomas and Miss Suffering but it was too late. She opened the drawer and it sprayed all over them. All four of us ran out of the room and now we're here. I tried to record as much as I could."

"Whoa! That's crazy!" Roxy said.

"I'm starting to see a pattern," Evan stated. He looked deep in thought. "Do you guys notice that these things are happening to Miss Suffering. It's almost as if someone has a vendetta against her."

"Not really. Maybe the slime. But the mice in the lunchroom that was for everyone," Shiloh surmised.

"Yeah, but it was during the time she's usually there. She always gets her lunch ten minutes into lunch period. It was timed perfectly."

"He's right. The stink bomb went off in Mr. Thomas' room and she's always in there too," Desirae agreed.

Evan considered this information. "Instead of trying to find The Watcher, maybe we should watch Miss Suffering."

Chapter Four
An Itch That Can't Be Scratched

The students were still outside trying to escape the stench of the stink bomb inside. Mingled with the students were firemen who were checking out groups of students making sure they were ok. The fire department had been called to investigate due to regulations. As the students milled around and talked, the teachers spoke to the firemen and recounted what happened. Miss Suffering who was standing next to Mr. Thomas whispered something to him and walked off.

Shiloh to Group:

> ```
> Cinderblock headed
> Evan's way.
> ```

Desirae to Group:

> ```
> We never decided
> her code name would
> be cinderblock.
> ```

Shiloh to Group:

> Cinderblock is
> perfect. She loves
> to wear gray and
> she's hard core
> like stone.

Desirae to Group:

> I like SilverFox
> better.

Shiloh to Group:

> SilverFox? That
> sounds all kinds of
> wrong.

Desirae to Group:

> You said she likes
> to wear gray.

Shiloh to Group:

> Exactly. Gray not
> silver.

Evan to Group:

> Can we focus? I see
> her. She's heading
> back inside.

Roxy to Group:

> What? Why would she
> go back in? It
> reeks in there.

Evan to Group:

> Where she goes we
> must follow.

Shiloh to Group:

> I'll keep watch out
> here.

Desirae to Group:

> Same.

Roxy to Group:

> Guys there's no
> point in staying
> outside when she's
> inside. Come on.
> Just put your face
> in your shirts.

```
Let's meet at the
entrance.
```

The four of them regrouped and followed her in. They spotted her walking towards her classroom and trailed her without her knowing. As she walked down the hall they heard her talking to herself.

"Be a teacher they said. It will be fun they said. Agony, you could've been a singer. You could be touring the country right now. *Oops, I did it again*." She started to sing her favorite song.

Roxy's hand just made it over Shiloh's mouth before he burst out laughing. "I can't help it. She sounds like a tone-deaf goat!" Shiloh whispered. Evan and Desirae also buried their heads further into their shirts to try and not laugh out loud. They dashed inside an open classroom before they were found.

Miss Suffering turned around quickly
and peered down the hall. "Hmm...I
could have sworn I heard
something. Agony, you're really
cracking up."

"I'm going to have to agree, she is
cracking up. She's talking to herself
and referring to herself in third
person," Desirae whispered from
the classroom they were hiding in.

"Shhh! I think I hear someone
coming!" Roxy said with her ear
against the door. "They're coming
this way! Hide–

As she whispered loudly for them to
hide the door was thrown open and

Roxy fell forward. Max caught her before she fell and stepped inside. Roxy stilled for a second in his arms and quickly got herself together. Max cleared his throat awkwardly.

"What are you doing here?" Evan asked.

"I was just about to ask you guys the same thing. I saw you all head inside and I thought I'd see what you guys were up to," Max said, a little too loud.

"Shhh! We're following Miss Suffering," Desirae said as she peered around the corner.

"Did I miss something?" Max asked.

"Yeah, we figured out that all the events always surround Miss Suffering so we reasoned that if we follow her she would lead us to The Watcher," Evan explained.

"Unless you're him. Then the case is closed," Shiloh stated matter-of-factly.

"For the last time, I am not The Watcher!" Max almost shouted.

"Ok! Keep your voice down!" Evan admonished.

"Guys! Miss Suffering didn't go to her classroom. She walked past it and went in the assembly hall," Desirae updated them.

"Let's go!" Evan said as he led them down the hall quietly.

They crouched down in front of the double doors and peered in the windows in the doors to see Miss Suffering standing on stage. She had changed out of her dirty gray dress and into another gray dress but this one had a big white bow at the collar. She stood still and stared at the microphone in her hand. All of a sudden, she started to dance around on stage and sing, "Oops, I did it again" over and over and over like a broken record.

"This is the weirdest thing I have ever seen and heard," Max declared.

The rest of them were speechless. They had never seen her crack a smile, sing, or dance. And now she was attempting all three. It was the most awkward, cringy thing they had ever seen. On top of that she started to scratch under her arms like a monkey.

"I think we should leave. I don't want to have to look her in the eye if she catches us," Roxy pitied her.

"Wait, look!" Evan said and pointed to her.

Her scratching had intensified into scratching everywhere and laying on the floor and scooting around trying to scratch her back.

"We should go in there and help her!" Roxy said.

"If we go in there, she's going to think we did it," Shiloh pointed out.

"We can't just leave her like this," Roxy said.

"She's right. C'mon," Evan agreed with Roxy.

They ran down the aisle of the amphitheater and jumped on stage.

"What do you kids want?" Miss Suffering asked while rolling around.

"We wanted to help you," Desirae said.

"Oh really? How did you know I was here?"

"Your beautiful singing lured us inside," Max said sarcastically.

"I could see that, but right now I can't be concerned with that. I need to get this thing off!"

Before they could stop her, she ripped off her dress.

The kids all gasped because they thought they were going to see her undressed, but true to form she had on what could only be described as an old-fashioned swimsuit with ruffles. The sleeves were long and the shorts went down to her knees. Underneath this she had on tights.

"I have to go shower in the locker room and get whatever is making me itch off of me!" She made as if to run but stopped and turned. "You five meet me in the principal's office in fifteen minutes. Don't be late!" She then turned and ran off.

Evan bent down to study the dress. There was evidence of white powder on the inside. "Guys, I think our theory is correct. I think this is itching powder. Someone's targeting these pranks towards Miss Suffering."

"Not someone, The Watcher," Desirae stated.

"I knew we were going to be blamed!" Shiloh complained.

"The weird thing is that we didn't have a puzzle to figure out or a note," Roxy wondered out loud.

"Maybe he didn't have time," Max shrugged.

Just then, they all got a text on their phones in a new group chat...with The Watcher.

Before you head to the principal's office I'd go down to the lab.

They looked at each other and gasped. "How did he get our numbers? Desirae exclaimed.

The next instant the doors to the amphitheater flew open and someone ran out. It was so fast that they only saw a shadow.

"He's here!" Max gasped.

"Let's get him!" Evan charged.

They all ran as fast as they could out into the hallway, but they didn't see anyone. It was silent.

"He can't be far," Desirae said.

"We'll end up wasting time if we try and look now. I say we go to the lab and see what the next clue is," Evan reasoned.

They nodded in agreement and headed down to the lab before their appointment with the principal

Chapter Five
Enough Is Enough

On the table in the lab was a puzzle and a note—again.

"I've had enough of these games, literally!" Shiloh yelled. "Do you hear me Watcher, I've had enough!"

"I gotta admit, usually I enjoy mysteries, but he has had us running around all day and I'm exhausted," Evan confessed.

"I can't believe I'm actually going to say this, but I miss just going to class," Max admitted.

"You guys are a bunch of babies. If the boys can't handle this, then leave it to us," Roxy said as Desirae nodded. They both rolled their eyes.

The boys looked embarrassed for complaining and got quiet.

Roxy started to assemble the puzzle while Desirae read the note.

I hope you guys had some fun
But unfortunately, this is the last one
I'll try and make it easy on you
See if you understand this clue
Monkeys and Weasels belong in a
zoo
But that isn't the only place you hear
about these two

The girls finished assembling the puzzle and didn't understand what they were looking at.

"It's some sort of tree," Desirae said as she stared.

"That's not a tree, it looks like a bush," Evan chimed in.

"If that's a bush then why is it so big?" Roxy asked.

"What are those red and purple things?" Shiloh pointed out.

"Some sort of fruit," Max answered.

"Guys, let's think about this while we meet with the principal. I don't want to get into any more trouble by being late," Shiloh was worried as he checked his phone for the time.

The five of them scrambled upstairs and slowed down just in front of the door so that they wouldn't look like they ran the whole way. Shiloh softly rapped on the door.

"Come in," a voice from inside directed.

Shiloh opened the door and they stepped inside to see Mr. Thomas seated behind a large desk with Miss Suffering standing next to him.

Mr. Thomas greeted them, "Hello students, two of you can sit while the rest of you stand."

The boys immediately stood behind the chairs to let the girls have the seats.

"I can stand," Desirae whispered to Evan.

"Don't be a hero. Just sit down so we can get this over with," Evan whispered back.

"As you know, I've been acting as the interim principal while we wait for our new principal to come later this month. Miss. Suffering has filled me in on what occurred over the last half hour. I have some questions," Mr. Thomas stated.

The kids weren't scared because Mr. Thomas was always nice to him, but they could feel the tension emanating from Miss Suffering.

"Why were you in the assembly hall when everyone was outside?" Mr. Thomas asked.

No one spoke at first, then everyone jumped in.

"Well you see—

"I wanted to go to the bathroom—

"I was going to my locker—

"I was just checking something—

Max said, "I heard this beautiful music—

"Ok, hold on everyone. One at a time. I'm very interested in your answer Max. You say you heard beautiful music?"

He nodded, "I couldn't believe what I was hearing so I came to check it out."

The rest of the gang looked at him in disbelief. Max made a face as if to tell them to follow his lead.

"Max, come now. There's no way that's true," Mr. Thomas guffawed.

"Well now, wait a second," Miss Suffering seemed very interested. "I was practicing my cover song."

"And it sounded so amazingly..." Max couldn't bring himself to lie anymore. "Awful!"

"Well!" She harrumphed, "I wouldn't expect you to know good music if it introduced itself and told you its life story!"

"Agony, I mean, Miss Suffering, calm down," Mr. Thomas admonished.

It always jarred Shiloh to remember that Miss Suffering's name was Agony, Agony Suffering. It was so weird but fitting.

"The question remains kids, what were you doing in there?" Mr. Thomas probed.

"Well, we wanted to come back in and see if the smell had faded," Desirae volunteered.

"How did you get a hold of my outfit and put itching powder in it?" Miss Suffering asked.

"We didn't do that. We have no idea who would do something like that," Roxy said.

"It's been quite a day. First the slime, then the mice, then the stink bomb, and now the itching powder. At all of these moments at least one or all of you were there," Miss suffering mused.

"Of course, because we all go to school here. It's impossible to avoid you, trust me I've tried." Max defended himself.

"Listen you little weasel!"

"Miss Suffering!" Mr. Thomas intervened. "They're still kids."

"I'm sorry but you guys are making my day horrible with all of these pranks!"

"Weasel...mulberry bush...monkeys...." Evan said softly under his breath.

Miss Suffering's head whipped around to Evan. "Evan?"

Shiloh thought that Evan must have been in some serious thought because he didn't even respond to Miss Suffering. He nudged Evan with his elbow to get him to come back to earth.

"Are we boring you?" The sarcasm was thick in Miss Suffering's voice.

"No ma'am, I was just thinking about weasels."

"At least you were listening."

"I've got it! Guys, I know what the puzzle meant." Evan was so excited, that he forgot he wasn't supposed to say anything in front of Miss Suffering and Mr. Thomas.

"Excuse me?" Mr. Thomas asked Evan, very confused.

"Ummm....we were working on puzzles..."

"That's a great hobby. Me and my mother do puzzles on the weekends. You guys should do puzzles with your mothers too. It'll keep you out of trouble." Miss Suffering nodded, agreeing with herself.

"Sounds fun...can we go?" Shiloh asked.

"Ok, but I'm warning you guys. I can't prove you guys are responsible for the pranks today but I can tell there's something that you're hiding. No more pranks. Got it?" Mr. Thomas gave each one of them a serious look.

"We would never—" Desirae tried to reassure him but got cut off.

Eerie music started to play over the speaker in the office. It was the speaker that was used to make school announcements in all of the classrooms and hallways.

"What in the world?" Miss Suffering marched to the door and opened it. The music was blaring in the hallway where students were gathering their books for the next class. They had been given the all clear to enter in again after the stink bomb so it was packed. Everyone looked at each other confused and creeped out.

Mr. Thomas and the gang followed her out of his office. While Mr. Thomas and Miss Suffering were distracted by the music, Evan beckoned his friends over.

"I know what the puzzle meant, but this means we need to look for something like a Jack-in-the-box."

"What?" Shiloh asked.

"I get it. The music." Roxy started to hum All Around The Mulberry Bush.

"That means, when the music stops something is going to pop out!" Shiloh looked around as if something was going to pop out right in front of him.

"I think we should leave. There's no way we're going to find it in time. The song is almost done!" Desirae said panicked.

As the song was in its last line it slowed down which increased the tension of the students who didn't know what else to do but stand there and listen. At the final note, no one spoke. It was as if they all held their breath.

Nothing happened.

A small giggle cut the tension, followed by a few more people softly laughing. Eventually everyone

broke out in full throated laughs.
Even Shiloh and his friends started
to laugh out of relief.

Then it happened.

The fire alarms started to go off and
all the sprinklers in the entire school
erupted. The laughing turned into
outright screams as people tried to
run back outside. But it was so full
that the students couldn't get out
fast enough so they were drenched
in seconds. As they tried to make
their way outside a few of them
slipped and fell on their behinds and
others tripped over them.

There was no place to hide. The
water was everywhere. Shiloh and
his friends had no choice but to go
outside too. Once again, there were

hundreds of students on the front lawn, but this time they were soaking wet. The firetrucks that had just left, now made a quick U-turn back.

"I give up," Max said as he laid on the ground.

"I agree. I just want to go home. My hair is ruined!" Desirae complained. What was once a pony-tail with laid edges was now a poof ball.

"It still looks nice to me," Evan tried to make her feel better. "I like when your hair is natural."

"I do too, when I style it that way! Not when buckets of water get poured on me." There was no calming her down.

As they sat down in the sun to dry, they discussed the clues and the possible suspects.

"It could be anyone. We don't have anything to go on. This will never end," Max whined.

"It won't go on forever. School is almost out and April Fools' Day will be over," Roxy answered, as if she was also trying to convince herself.

"I've got an idea! I have all of the footage. I'll make a TikTok account and upload all of it and pretend to take all of the credit." Shiloh took out his phone and got started.

"Wait, you can't do that. You'll get in trouble for something you didn't do." Desirae put her hand on his arm.

Evan cleared his throat loudly making Shiloh slightly move his arm away from Desirae. "Actually, that's a great idea. We can do it anonymously. In fact, we'll call it The Watcher. Maybe if we do that, he'll get upset and try and take credit for it and reveal something that will lead us to him."

"Let's start giving him puzzles!" Roxy was getting excited. "Well maybe not puzzles, but messages. Those puzzles took too long."

"Yeah! Let's make him reveal himself or...wait, what do we have that will make him reveal himself?" Max asked.

"Let's say we know who it is and it will be revealed to everyone if he doesn't come clean to us," Shiloh said. "We'll turn the tables on him. How does he know that we don't know?"

"Shiloh, I thought you said you had to delete the slime prank?" Roxy asked.

"I did, but I don't think Miss Suffering understands how to work a phone completely. It saved in my deleted folder." He smirked. "Ok, I made the account and I'm going to upload them all now."

"Alright it's done." He announced.

They gathered around and started to see all the videos rack up thousands of views in seconds.

"It's definitely going viral," Roxy stated.

"Ok, now what?" Max asked.

"We wait. We'll monitor the comments and see if he says anything. Let's also get down to the lab and think of our next step." Evan got up to go.

Desirae stopped him. "But what if it's soaking wet in there? We just dried out."

"It won't be wet. Because it was an old bunker from the Cold War, it has a different utility system than the rest of the school." Evan put out his hand to help her up.

~

As they sat around the lab, they watched videos on their phones. They were bored and tired. They always looked forward to school ending but today they especially wanted the day to end.

"Guys we have a hit," Shiloh announced.

Chapter Six
The Real Official Watcher

The group gathered around Shiloh's phone and read the comment.

TikTok comments:

> *therealofficialwatcher*
> How dare you take my name and credit for my pranks?

"Hmmm, looks like he's upset. Look at the name." Shiloh laughed.

"We should respond," Roxy suggested.

> *thewatcher*
> How dare you say they're your pranks? Clearly, I planned all of them and that's why I have footage. You have no proof they're yours.

A few seconds later...

therealofficialwatcher
I have proof. I can prove I did them all. Take down this account and I will show you.

thewatcher
No way. It's gone viral now. The videos all have millions of views. Go away and make your own account and stop trying to get clout from our page before we report you as a copy account and spammer.

randomdude20
Yeah bruh, stop trying to get clout. You're a clout chaser.

The Watcher to Group Chat:

Take it down now!

"Ooooh, he's big mad!" Shiloh laughed, as he read the text on his phone.

The Watcher to Group Chat:

> What do you want in
> order to take it
> down? I'll do
> anything but reveal
> myself.

Shiloh to Group Chat and Watcher:

> No. That's the
> deal. Reveal
> yourself and tell
> us why you did all
> of this and why you
> did the ciphers
> last fall, or else
> we get all the
> clout. And all the
> pranks you do from
> here on in, we'll
> take the credit.

There was no response.

"Do you think I asked for too much?" Shiloh looked around at his friends.

"No. Go big or go home. At this rate we have nothing to lose," Desirae shrugged.

"Besides, I think I have a plan. I'm going to triangulate his position from the IP address he used to make the comments on TikTok. I can't believe I didn't think of this before!" Evan face-palmed himself.

"Dude chill, we literally put up the TikTok account like ten minutes ago," Shiloh reassured him.

"I know, but I could've trapped him earlier with this plan." Evan got up and went to his computer and started to input codes and numbers. The rest of them just stood and stared. This was Evan's specialty. His gadgets and computer skills always came through.

"Guys, you're never going to believe this. It's the IP of the school. The Watcher is still here. I have a coin finder I use to find coins in the sand. If I could recalibrate it to search for signals, we can locate where he's hiding using the device." Evan started to unscrew the main panel. "Keep him talking on TikTok."

TikTok comments:

> *thewatcher*
> who wants to see more pranks? I made these awesome puzzles and messages.

> *therealofficialwatcher*
> I MADE THOSE TOO. DON'T LISTEN TO HIM

> *Randomdude20*
> why are you still here? We wanna see more pranks

> *thewatcher*
> I can teach you all how to do these pranks and you can

make your own watcher
accounts. Who's in?

The Watcher to Group Text:

> Ok. I agree to the
> terms.

"He agrees to the terms," Shiloh
announced to the group. "I don't
trust him. We should still do Evan's
plan."

"It's almost ready. Give me a few
more minutes."

TikTok comments:

> *thewatcher*
> So for the first prank, all you
> need is a phone, slime, and a
> bucket.

The Watcher to Group Text:

> Why are you still
> talking on TikTok?
> I agreed to the
> terms.

"He wants to know why we're still talking on TikTok?" Shiloh told the group,

"It's ready. Tell him we'll stop once he reveals himself so he better do it fast," Evan answered.

Shiloh to Group Text and The Watcher:

> We'll stop once you
> reveal yourself.
> Meet us in the
> assembly hall. No
> funny tricks.

The Watcher to Group Text:

> When?

"Evan how fast will that thing work?" Shiloh asked.

"The school's not that big so give me ten minutes. Des, come with me. Roxy, you and Max go to the assembly hall and Shiloh you stay here in case he tries to come in here to leave some sort of puzzle again," Evan ordered.

The group split up while Shiloh
continued to talk to The Watcher on
TikTok and in texts.

Shiloh to Group text and The
Watcher:

> In ten minutes.

The Watcher to Group Text:

> Alright, but MY
> terms are that you
> have to admit that
> these pranks are
> mine on your
> TikTok, and that
> you wanted my
> clout. Then you
> need to delete your
> account.

TikTok comments:

> *thewatcher*
> I have an important
> announcement to make.

> *randomdude20*
> You have another prank??

A few minutes passed. Shiloh waited
to see if he heard anything from
Desirae and Evan.

Shiloh to Group Text and The
Watcher:

> Are you almost at
> the assembly hall?

No response.

Shiloh to Group Text and The
Watcher:

> Hello?

A rattling sound behind the door
startled Shiloh. He went rigid for a
second and stayed absolutely still to
see if he heard it again. Another
rattle, but a lot louder. Shiloh raced
to the door and opened it only to
see the edge of a black cape fly up
the stairs. Shiloh gave chase and ran
into the main hallway. He heard
footsteps run in the direction of the
assembly hall.

As he ran to the assembly hall he
bumped into Evan and Desirae who

appeared out of breath like they also ran over. The three of them stood in front of the doors to catch their breath. The doors flung open and Max and Roxy spilled out.

"Where did he go?" Max yelled out.

"We thought he went in to the assembly hall. My signal said he was here," Evan answered.

"I heard rattling outside of the lab door and I went to see what it was and I saw the edge of a black cape and I ran after him," Shiloh said confused.

"We heard a commotion out here and we thought it was him so we ran out," Roxy said.

The Watcher to Group Text:

        I'm here.

The lights went out in the assembly hall and the spotlight illuminated the stage but no one was there. The five of them went inside and walked slowly down to the stage. They stood there and looked around and waited.

"I'm right here." A robot manipulated voice boomed through the speaker. The Watcher was in the sound room. "Don't try and come up here because I'll be gone before you make it to the stairs."

The five of them couldn't see because of the spotlight. All they could do was stand there and listen.

"Today was almost everything I wanted. You see it was on this day many years ago I had a prank done on me. Before TikTok, there was something called Facebook. If you don't know what that is, ask your parents. Someone rigged a lemon meringue pie to get me in the face when I opened my locker and they posted it on Facebook. It was delicious, but I was—

"Humiliated?" Shiloh offered.

"No, I was a star! I never had so many people wanting to know who I was. Before that day I was invisible and now I was cool. I guess I enjoyed it too much because Miss Suffering accused me of doing it to myself. Can you believe that? Why would I smash a pie in my own face? After that, I was labeled a fake. I tried to convince everyone that it was real but no one believed me. After that, no one ever pranked me again. I blame Miss Suffering!"

"So that's why you targeted her?" Desirae asked.

"I wanted her to see how awesome it was to have all that attention."

"I don't think that's how she saw it," Shiloh said.

"I was going to put it on TikTok and make her a star and then rip it away from her by saying she did it to herself. I didn't want her to know it was me and you guys were a convenient group to blame since you guys seem like you're a bunch of busybodies. Unfortunately, you guys put it up and now my plan has been ruined. I'm labeled a fake again, but now on TikTok!"

"But what you did was mean and affected the entire school. You also got us in trouble because she thinks it's us." Roxy was looked very irritated.

"No, I know it wasn't any of you." Miss Suffering said as she and Mr. Thomas walked on stage. "Percy come down here right now!" She called to the stage. "And turn on these lights."

"This isn't Percy. This is The Watcher!" The robot voice answered with a slight tremor in its voice.

"Percival Simmons come down right now! I know it's you from your little sob story! Don't let me have to come up there," she threatened.

"Yes ma'am! I'm coming down right now!" The lights came on and they heard some scuffling.

"Percival graduated from Cornerstone ten years ago. He was always strange but smart. I guess strange plus smart equals this weird day we had today," she sighed.

A small figure in a black hood and cape quickly walked down the aisle toward the stage. Shiloh and his friends just stared. When he got to the stage Miss Suffering marched up to him and yanked off his hood.

"You are in big trouble mister!" Miss Suffering said.

"I was just joking around! I'm sorry! Please forgive me!" Percival begged.

Mr. Thomas looked angry. The kids had never seen him look so upset. "Tell me why we should forgive you. You have not only wasted everyone's day today, but you also put people in danger. The stench from the stink bomb got some people sick. The water in the hallway made it slippery and some fell and the mice in the lunchroom is a health hazard! Young man, these weren't harmless. You went too far. We're going to the police."

"Oh no! Mr. Thomas please forgive me! I'm sorry. I won't do it again." Percival got on his knees.

"Tell that to the cops." Mr. Thomas wasn't budging as he started drag him off stage.

"Wait," Miss Suffering stopped Mr. Thomas. "He said he was sorry. I didn't know that all those years ago I embarrassed you. I'm sorry too, but that's no excuse for today. If you're truly sorry then I forgive you."

"Thanks Miss Suffering! I never knew you could be so nice!" He exclaimed.

Shiloh thought the same thing as he watched their interaction.

"To make it up to me and the whole school you are going to help clean every inch of this school and fix anything that's broken. If you don't we'll report you. And since you clearly need a life, you can come by this weekend and do puzzles with me and my mother."

"But—

Miss Suffering arched her brow, waiting to hear the rest of his sentence.

"Ok." Percival put his head down.

"You five, go home and get some rest. School's over," Miss Suffering ordered. She and Mr. Thomas walked on either side of Percival as they started to make a list of all the things he had to fix and clean.

"Wow! I wasn't expecting that," Max looked surprised.

"Me either," Roxy said.

Suddenly Shiloh felt exhausted. He was more than ready to go home.

"Guys it's been such a long day. I gotta go. I'll see you tomorrow."

Chapter Seven
Freight Train Remix

Later that night, after a long nap, Shiloh woke up to a ding from his phone. He rolled over and picked it up from the nightstand.

Roxy to Shiloh:

> Are you up?

Shiloh to Roxy:

> I am now

Roxy to Shiloh:

Oops. I was just going to say
sorry for getting upset earlier today.

Shiloh to Roxy:

It's ok. That seems like ages
ago. Besides, I'm sorry for
not paying more attention to
our conversation.

Roxy to Shiloh:

I want to ask you
something.

Shiloh got nervous all of a sudden.
He sat up in his bed and his palms
started to get sweaty.

Shiloh to Roxy:

Ok...

Roxy to Shiloh:

Do you think that
we need to buy new
phones because
Percival was
somehow able to get
our numbers?

Shiloh exhaled loudly. He didn't even know he was holding his breath. He couldn't explain why he got nervous for a second but all he felt now was relief.

Shiloh to Roxy:

> I asked Evan and he said he would get us new SIM cards that he would get and he was going to put something in to also make it even more secure. It pays to have a technician for a best friend.

Roxy to Shiloh:

> I wonder if anyone else is up.

Desirae to Shiloh:

> Hey...

Shiloh to Desirae:

> Hey. I think Roxy
> is up. Let's go to
> the group chat.

Desirae to Shiloh:

> Wait, I just want
> to say I'm sorry
> for getting upset
> earlier.

Shiloh to Desirae:

> Me too. It's
> complicated...Evan'
> s my best friend

Desirae to Shiloh:

> He's also one of my
> best friends too...

Evan to Group Chat:

> Anyone awake? Don't
> you think it's
> crazy how Percival
> was able to sneak
> into the lab and
> get our numbers and
> set up all those

elaborate pranks.
Would it be weird
if I ask him to
work with me? We
could create some
really cool stuff.
What do you guys
think?

Max to Group Chat:

I'm awake, but I
feel like you maybe
you're talking in
your sleep. Why
would anyone want
to work with that
weirdo? You're
asking for trouble.

Roxy to Group Chat:

No. Way.

Desirae to Group Chat:

You should probably
go back to sleep
Evan, clearly
you're still tired
and not thinking
straight.

Shiloh enjoyed the jokes for the next couple of hours before they all gradually fell asleep again. It was late but he decided he couldn't let the day pass before getting his sister back. He thought he was all pranked out but decided that he still had one more in him.

He quietly opened the door to her room and saw her sleeping. Shiloh had told her that she snored like a freight train, but she refused to believe him. Well, he thought, she was going to believe him now. He recorded her sleeping for a couple of minutes and then slipped out quietly. He posted it on his TikTok and let the app do its work.

~

The next morning he was awakened by a scream, "SHILOH! OPEN YOUR DOOR!"

Shiloh thought it was a good thing that he locked his door before he went to sleep. He opened up his phone to see that her snoring went viral. It went so viral that there was already a remix of it. He rolled over to catch a few more minutes of sleep. His work was done.

The End.

Acknowledgments

I want to thank my family again for their support. Your continual affirmation and encouragement is what keeps me going. I love you.

About the Author

Rita Onyx is a member of the Onyx Family who also include Mirthell, Shalom, Sinead, Shasha, and Shiloh. Together they have a successful social media and YouTube following with over 4 million subscribers and over 1 billion views across their channels. You can find them on Onyx Flix and YouTube.

Other Onyx Kids Books:

Onyx Kids School Days:
The Sealed Locker
The Class Pet Fraud
The Phantom of the School Play
The Secret Santa
The Secret Admirer
The Spooky Cipher

Onyx Kids Adventures:
Don't Leave the Door Open
Headless Horseman
Kidnapped by a Dragon
Zombie Outbreak
Pop Me If You Dare
'Twas the Fright Before Christmas
Welcome to the Prey Ground
Eat or Be Eaten
Kitchen Kreepers
Ahoy Danger
Valentine Villain
The Unlucky Leprechaun
Hybrid Horsey

Getting to Know Onyx Kids

Made in the USA
Monee, IL
07 July 2021

73122832R00069